# To the IDF צה״ל

At school, Shira learned all about the holiday of Chanukah חֲנֻכָּה, the holy temple in Jerusalem בֵּית הַמִקְדָּשׁ, the Maccabees מַכַּבִּים , the Greeks יְוָנִים, the menorah מְנוֹרָה, and the small jug of oil כַּד שֶׁמֶן that by a miracle נֵס lasted for eight days instead of one.

Her teacher told the story about the fight of few against many, how light won over darkness, and good overcame evil. They learned about lighting the CHANUKIAH חֲנֻכִּיָּה with the blessings, singing songs, making jelly doughnuts סֻפְגָּנִיּוֹת and latkes לְבִיבוֹת that are fried in oil, to remind us of the miracle נֵס of the oil.

2

3

Chanukiah

Menorah

4

They played SEVIVON סְבִיבוֹן games, where each player gets five chocolate coins and the rest goes to the bank, in the middle.

נ NUN gets nothing from the chocolate coin bank, ג GIMMEL gets all the bank, ה HEY gets half the coins and when the SEVIVON סְבִיבוֹן lands on ש SHIN, the player puts one coin back into the bank.

She also learned the difference between a MENORAH מְנוֹרָה and a CHANUKIAH חֲנֻכִּיה.

A Menorah has seven branches and is an ancient Jewish symbol, while a CHANUKIAH חֲנֻכִּיה is a nine branch candelabra, especially designed to commemorate the miracle of the oil שֶׁמֶן lasting eight days.

5

At home, Shira told her parents the Chanukah חֲנֻכָּה story and taught them a holiday song:

בָּאנוּ חוֹשֶׁךְ לְגָרֵשׁ

בְּיָדֵינוּ אוֹר וָאֵשׁ

כֹּל אֶחָד הוּא אוֹר קָטָן

וְכוּלָנוּ - אוֹר אֵיתָן

סוּרָה חוֹשֶׁךְ, הָלְאָה שְׁחוֹר

סוּרָה מִפְּנֵי הָאוֹר

Just before dinner, her mom said, "I almost forgot! Your Aunt Hannah דּוֹדָה חָנָה, sent you a package from Israel and it arrived today in the mail. Go open it; it is by the fireplace."

Shira ran to the living room, picked up the package, and shook it gently. She thought, "I wonder what's inside the package?" Carefully she opened the box; she saw a note from her aunt דּוֹדָה that read:

Dear Shira, my sweet, fantastic niece,

I hope this gift will make the holiday of Chanukah interesting and fun for you. May miracles happen to you on this festival of lights.

Love always,
DODA Hannah  דּוֹדָה חַנָּה
from Jerusalem, Israel.

Shira smiled. She loved and missed her aunt very much and could not wait to see what she had sent her all the way from Israel.

8

One by one Shira removed the tissue papers, until she saw, at the bottom of the box, a SEVIVON סְבִיבוֹן spinning top, with the letters נ NUN, ג GIMMEL, ה HEY, and פ PE? Shira looked carefully at the SEVIVON סְבִיבוֹן and then called her mom, "Mom, DODA דוֹדָה Hannah sent me a weird SEVIVON סְבִיבוֹן !!! This is wrong; there should be a שׁ SHIN instead of the letter פ PE... "

Her mother smiled and explained, "In Israel the SEVIVON סְבִיבוֹן has the letters for נֵס גָּדוֹל הָיָה פֹּה --NES GADOL HAYA PO - a great miracle happened here, and a SEVIVON סְבִיבוֹן from here has נֵס גָּדוֹל הָיָה שָׁם --NES GADOL HAYA SHAM - a great miracle happened there!"

" Ahhh... " Shira answered, "I get it... The spinning tops are different in Israel because the miracle happened over there! This is a very special SEVIVON סְבִיבוֹן; none of my friends has this kind of SEVIVON סְבִיבוֹן from Israel. I will take it to class tomorrow to show everyone."

11

The next day, Shira stood in front of her class, next to her teacher, and explained the letters on her Israeli SEVIVON סְבִיבוֹן. All the children in the class were impressed, and asked to play with Shira's unusual SEVIVON סְבִיבוֹן. They did, and soon after, the teacher said, "Tonight is the first night of Chanukah! Everybody, please gather by the window to light the CHANUKIAH חֲנֻכִּיָּה. Shira, would you like to put your special SEVIVON סְבִיבוֹן for display next to our jug of oil כַּד שֶׁמֶן, the candle box, the blessings page, and our class CHANUKIAH חֲנֻכִּיָּה?"
Shira replied happily," Sure, my new Israeli SEVIVON סְבִיבוֹן will look just right next to our class CHANUKIAH חֲנֻכִּיָּה."

12

They all recited the blessings:

בָּרוּךְ אַתָּה ה , אֱלוֹהֵינוּ מֶלֶךְ הָעוֹלָם,

אֲשֶׁר קִדְּשָׁנוּ בְמִצְוֹתָיו, וְצִוָּנוּ לְהַדְלִיק נֵר שֶׁל חֲנֻכָּה.

בָּרוּךְ אַתָּה ה , אֱלוֹהֵינוּ מֶלֶךְ הָעוֹלָם,

שֶׁעָשָׂה נִסִּים לַאֲבוֹתֵינוּ, בְּיָמִים הָהֵם בַּזְּמַן הַזֶּה.

בָּרוּךְ אַתָּה ה , אֱלוֹהֵינוּ מֶלֶךְ הָעוֹלָם,

שֶׁהֶחֱיָינוּ, וְקִיְּמָנוּ, וְהִגִּיעָנוּ לַזְּמַן הַזֶּה

Then, they lit one candle with
the SHAMASH (helper) שַׁמָּשׁ , sang
holiday songs, and ate SOOFGANIYOT
סֻפְגָנִיּוֹת (jelly doughnuts).
13

On the second day of Chanukah, Shira and all her classmates gathered by the window to light the CHANUKIAH חֲנֻכִּיָּה to celebrate the second night of Chanukah. Shira noticed the CHANUKIAH חֲנֻכִּיָּה, the candle box, the blessings page, the small jug of oil כַּד שֶׁמֶן - but where was her special SEVIVON סְבִיבוֹן? Where was her Israeli SEVIVON סְבִיבוֹן from her Aunt Hannah דּוֹדָה חָנָה? GONE!

She looked at her teacher and asked, "Have you seen my SEVIVON סְבִיבוֹן?" She looked at her friends and asked, "Where is my Israeli SEVIVON סְבִיבוֹן? It was right here yesterday. Did anybody take it?" No one did! No one knew where the SEVIVON סְבִיבוֹן was; it was lost! Shira asked her teacher, "May I check in 'Lost and Found'?"

Her teacher replied, "Sure."

14

Shira made her way to 'Lost and Found', but there was nothing there. Back in class she was worried, but her teacher reassured her, "We will keep looking; I hope your SEVIVON סְבִיבוֹן will turn up soon."

On the third day of Chanukah חֲנֻכָּה the classes gathered by the window, lit the CHANUKIAH חֲנֻכִּיָּה, recited the blessings, sang songs and ate latkes לְבִיבוֹת. Shira's SEVIVON סְבִיבוֹן was still missing. Shira asked, "May I check the lobby?" 17

Her teacher nodded and Shira went to look for her SEVIVON סְבִיבוֹן in the lobby. There was no SEVIVON סְבִיבוֹן there. The receptionist told Shira she had not seen an Israeli SEVIVON סְבִיבוֹן.

In class the teacher looked at Shira's disappointed face and said,
"Don't be discouraged, okay?"

The fourth and fifth nights were the weekend, no school, but Shira was concerned, thinking about her lost SEVIVON סְבִיבוֹן, somewhere in the school building...

On the sixth day of Chanukah חֲנֻכָּה, the class gathered by the window, lit the CHANUKIAH חֲנֻכִּיה , recited the blessings, sang songs, and ate chocolate coins. No Israeli SEVIVON סְבִיבוֹן was in sight...

Shira asked her teacher, "May I check the gym? Maybe my SEVIVON סְבִיבוֹן is there?" Her teacher clapped and responded, "Great idea, go ahead, check the gym." Shira went to the gym, looked everywhere, and even asked the coach if he had seen an Israeli SEVIVON סְבִיבוֹן.

There was no SEVIVON סְבִיבוֹן in the gym. Back in class Shira's face was sad. Her teacher comforted her and said, "It will show up ... I hope."

On the seventh day of Chanukah חֲנֻכָּה, the class gathered by the window, lit the CHANUKIAH חֲנֻכִּיָּה, recited the blessings, sang songs, and ate latkes לְבִיבוֹת, but still no SEVIVON סְבִיבוֹן appeared. Shira asked: "May I check the cafeteria? I really hope the SEVIVON סְבִיבוֹן is there."

Hopeful, Shira went to the cafeteria and looked everywhere, including under the tables... She described her lost SEVIVON סְבִיבוֹן to the lunch lady, but with no luck. Shira returned to class with tears in her eyes. "My SEVIVON סְבִיבוֹן is gone and Chanukah is almost over."

Her friends hugged her and her teacher said, "Keep believing, Shira, keep believing!"

23

On the eighth day of Chanukah חֲנֻכָּה, the last day, the class gathered by the window. The teacher asked Shira to place the candles on the CHANUKIAH חֲנֻכִּיָּה from right to left, which she did. One after another Shira removed the candles from the big candle box and placed them on the class CHANUKIAH חֲנֻכִּיָּה. When she put her hand into the box to remove the eighth candle, she felt something! She pulled it out; it was her Israeli SEVIVON סְבִיבוֹן!

24

Shira held it up and started
dancing around the room shouting,

"NES GADOL HAYA PO!
נֵס גָּדוֹל הָיָה פֹּה
A great miracle happened here!
I found my Israeli SEVIVON, סְבִיבוֹן
נֵס גָּדוֹל הָיָה פֹּה
NES GADOL HAYA PO!"

Her classmates danced with her, and
the teacher joined in the celebration.
Later, they all played SEVIVON
סְבִיבוֹן games with Shira's special
Israeli SEVIVON סְבִיבוֹן.

26

27

That night Shira Skyped her Aunt Hannah דּוֹדָה חָנָה in Israel and told her about the miracle נֵס story that had happened with her special SEVIVON סְבִיבוֹן.

DODA Hannah דּוֹדָה חָנָה answered, "Shira, my dear, miracles do happen... they do!"

חַג שָׂמֵחַ
CHAG SAMEACH!!!

29

The story behind the story:

The author, Galia Sabbag, is a veteran Hebrew teacher of over fifteen years at The Davis Academy, a Reform Jewish Day School in Atlanta, GA. During her years of teaching, she has come across some beautiful, thought-provoking examples of how school affects families and their home life and how children grow in Jewish knowledge and spirituality. By witnessing these "aha" moments and/or by listening to parents' and grandparents' anecdotes, a series of stories emerged, and became lovable "Shira." She is the culmination of all Mrs. Sabbag's students throughout the years. Most of the stories in the series are real ones that actually happened to real students, interwoven with the author's creativity. The miracles, in all their beautiful variety, that happen every day in her own classroom, are what inspired Galia Sabbag to write about Shira's own wondrous miracle.

Mrs. Sabbag's stories are imbued with and enriched by Hebrew words, songs, greetings, and blessings. These stories will appeal to children in Jewish preschools, Sunday school or Jewish day schools and of course, in every Jewish home.

Coming soon in the series:
*Shira in the Sukkah* - a Sukkot Story
*Shira and the Torah* - a Simchat Torah Story
*Shira and the Trees*- a Tu Bishvat Story
and many, many more....

If you enjoyed *Miracle for Shira* you will love other stories in the Shira series: *Shira in the Temple* and *RIMON for Shira*. The eBooks are available on Amazon Kindle and on Barnes and Noble Nook. Printed copies are available through the website.

Please check out the website:
www.shirasseries.com
twitter: @shirasSeries
or the facebook page: www.Facebook.com/Shira.series

Made in the USA
Lexington, KY
10 December 2014